THE WORLD'S
STICKIEST EARWAX

Steve Hartley is a sensible man. He has a sensible job, a sensible family, lives in a sensible house and drives a sensible car. But underneath it all, he longs to be silly. There have been occasional forays into silliness: Steve has been a football mascot called Desmond Dragon, and has tasted World Record success himself – taking part in both a mass yodel and a mass yo-yo. But he wanted more, and so his alter ego – Danny Baker Record Breaker – was created. Steve lives in Lancashire with his wife and teenage daughter.

You can find out more about Steve on his extremely silly website:
www.stevehartley.net

Books by Steve Hartley

DANNY BAKER RECORD BREAKER
The World's Biggest Bogey

DANNY BAKER RECORD BREAKER
The World's Awesomest Air-Barf

DANNY BAKER RECORD BREAKER
The World's Loudest Armpit Fart

DANNY BAKER RECORD BREAKER
The World's Stickiest Earwax

Look out for more
Danny Baker books
coming soon!

STEVE HARTLEY

DANNY BAKER RECORD BREAKER

THE WORLD'S
STICKIEST EARWAX

ILLUSTRATED BY KATE PANKHURST

MACMILLAN CHILDREN'S BOOKS

First published 2010 by Macmillan Children's Books
a division of Macmillan Publishers Limited
20 New Wharf Road, London N1 9RR
Basingstoke and Oxford
Associated companies throughout the world
www.panmacmillan.com

ISBN 978-0-330-50919-0

Text copyright © Steve Hartley 2010
Illustrations copyright © Kate Pankhurst 2010

The right of Steve Hartley and Kate Pankhurst to be identified as the
author and illustrator of this work has been asserted by them in
accordance with the Copyright, Designs and Patents Act 1988.

1 3 5 7 9 8 6 4 2

A CIP catalogue record for this book is available from
the British Library.

Printed and bound in the UK by CPI Mackays Chatham ME5 8TD

For Rosie

DANNY BAKER RECORD BREAKER

The Highland
Fling

The SweatSucker

To the Keeper of the Records
The Great Big Book of World Records
London

Dear Mr Bibby

Last weekend, my swimming club, the Penleydale
Sea Squirts, had a day out at Bladderpool
Pleasure Dome. I took The SweatSucker
Challenge, and won! I rode this rollercoaster
that's so fast and scary, it makes you sweat
buckets! But when I went through the moisture-
meter at the end, I was as dry as a desert
in a dry spell. It hadn't sucked
MY sweat! I got free goes, and
stayed un-sweaty for twenty-five
rides before the Pleasure Dome
people made me stop. They gave
me a Certificate of Dryness
AND free admission to the park
for life! Ace!

sweaty

moisture-
meter

dry

My best friend Matthew's sweat got really sucked. He was drenched. My sister, Natalie, and the other girls in the swimming club wouldn't go on it at all, because they don't think being sweaty is fun. Unluckily for them, when everyone's sweat got sucked on the fantastic reverse-triple-spiral-corkscrew-loop-the-loop, they were standing underneath and they got soaked!

sweat

I know I'm not the first to beat The SweatSucker, but has anyone else ever gone for twenty-five rides and stayed sweat-free?

Best wishes
Danny Baker

The Great Big Book
of World Records
London

ARE YOU A RECORD
BREAKER ?

Dear Danny

The first person ever to beat The SweatSucker
also registered the Most Consecutive Rides
without Sweating. On 21 July 2007, Didier
Tremblay, of Quebec in Canada, managed to
complete 157 consecutive rides and not sweat
a single drop. However, nobody realized that
Didier had cheated! Before going on The
SweatSucker, he had covered his entire body
in Industrial Strength Antiperspirant. When
he took a shower and washed it off three
days later, all the pent-up sweat burst out
of every pore in his skin, as though he had
been punctured by millions of needles. Didier
collapsed dead in the bathtub, his shrivelled
body lying like a squeezed-out sponge in an
enormous pool of his own smelly sweat.

Since then, Bladderpool Pleasure Dome has limited successful riders to a maximum of twenty-five sweat-free goes. However, you are only the third person to have achieved this amazing feat! You are now twenty-five per cent of the way to completing the TerrorCoaster Grand Slam: taking on and beating the Top Four Rollercoaster Rides in the country (as voted for by the readers of *Cool Coasters Quarterly*).

The SweatSucker is in fourth place. The top three, in reverse order, are:

The brand-new BoneShaker at Tartan Towers Holiday Park, Saltimuchty, Scotland. It claims to shake your bones right out of your skin! So far, only two riders (0.00374%) have been able to stand up and walk the straight 10-m line at the end.

The BarfMaker at Ballynoggin's Leprechaun Leap Fun Centre, Northern Ireland. Drink your

'Compulsory Super-thick Banana Milkshake'
before you ride, and then try NOT to barf! This
rollercoaster is so whirly and swirly that so
far nobody (0.00000%) has been able to keep
their milkshake down!

And finally, the Most Awesome Rollercoaster in
Great Britain: The Pontypyddl PantWetter at Red
Dragonland in Wales, a ride so *seriously scary*,
it's *guaranteed* to make you wet your pants!

You could become the first person *ever* to ride
all four rollercoasters and not sweat, wobble,
vomit or wee! Go for it, Danny!

Best wishes
Eric Bibby
Keeper of the Records

Danny, Natalie, Mum and Dad drove home after spending a day out in the village of Pugswallop, at the 46th Annual World Rice-pudding-wrestling Championships.

'What a waste of a Sunday!' moaned Natalie.

'Be fair, Nat,' said Danny. 'I spent all last Sunday watching you swim up and down a pool in the County Swimming Trials. The least you can do is spend an afternoon watching me wrestle in rice pudding!'

'You didn't even win!'

'It was my first try!' protested Danny. 'The lad who beat me pudding-wrestles for Wales!'

His sister sniffed. 'At least you smell a bit sweeter than you normally do!'

Mum turned on the radio. The sound of Natalie's favourite boy band filled the car.

'Fab!' cried Natalie, and began to sing. '*Yooooooou are my one and only girrrrrl. Ooooooooooo, bay-bee.*'

'I can burp this song,' announced Danny, joining in with loud, ringing belches.

Natalie pulled a face. 'You're such a *child*!' she

sneered, sticking her fingers in her ears.

Soon they arrived in Penleydale. Dad turned on to the road over Hangman's Hump and they began to descend into Burly Bottoms.

'Mum! Tell him!' said Natalie. 'Danny's reading a book!'

'Excellent!' replied Mum.

'He's only trying to make himself carsick so he can break some disgusting record, like . . . Completely Filling a Car with Vomit!'

'Ace idea, Nat!' laughed Danny. 'I wonder what the record is.'

'Stop bickering, you two!' ordered Mum. 'If you keep this up over the half-term holiday, you'll drive

me mad! The doctor said I have to rest now that the baby's nearly here.'

'I'll go mad with boredom,' said Natalie. 'Kaylie and Kylie are going to Tenerife next week. What am *I* going to do?'

'You can play footy with me and Matt,' suggested Danny.

'As if!'

Walking through their front door, they heard the telephone ring and Dad hurried into the kitchen to answer it.

Mum, Danny and Natalie went into the living room. The floor was strewn with old baby things:

plastic toys and tiny clothes, a pushchair, a potty and a dismantled cot.

Mum sat down, rummaged through a box and held up two little mittens, one pink and one blue.

'I wonder which of these I'll be using for the new baby,' she said.

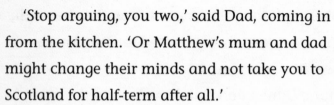

'Pink,' said Natalie. 'It's *totally* going to be a girl.'

'Blue,' said Danny. 'It's *got* to be a boy.'

'Stop arguing, you two,' said Dad, coming in from the kitchen. 'Or Matthew's mum and dad might change their minds and not take you to Scotland for half-term after all.'

'What?!' cried the children.

'The rollercoaster at Tartan Towers has gone on the blink,' he explained. 'Matthew's dad's going up to Scotland on Saturday to fix it. They thought they'd give your mum a break over the holidays and take you two with them.'

'Ace!' exclaimed Danny. 'Mr Bibby says The BoneShaker's the third best ride in Britain! It must be *really* brilliant if it beats The SweatSucker.'

Natalie gave a small growl. 'So I have to spend

all next week
with him and
Matthew?'

'Are you coming,
Dad?' asked Danny.

'No, I can't get
away from work,'
Dad replied. 'We're

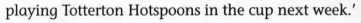

playing Totterton Hotspoons in the cup next week.'

'That's settled then,' said Mum. 'You'd both
better start packing.'

Are We Nearly There Yet?

Dear Mr Bibby

Guess what? I'm going to take on The BoneShaker at Tartan Towers, once Matthew's dad's mended it. He's a Rollercoaster Fixer – what an Ace Job!

We'll be camping there for a week, and I've packed for a record – Alphabetical Suitcase Packing. I've stuck to the rules. I'm going to Saltimuchty in Scotland, so I've filled my bag with twenty-five things that start with the letter 'S'. It's been really hard! My skateboard was too big to go in. The stuffed snake my Grandad Nobby gave me for Christmas is slowly shedding its skin. My spider collection has got lost somewhere in the junk in my bedroom (I'm

taking a plastic spider
instead — I hope that still
counts).

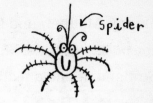
spider

I've sent a list of what I
have packed in my case. One letter down, only
twenty-five to go!

Best wishes
Danny Baker

PS My address for the next week will be: Tartan
Towers Holiday Park, Saltimuchty, Scotland.

Danny, Matthew and Natalie were squashed into the back seat of the Masons' car on the way to Scotland. It had already been a very long journey for Natalie. The boys had played I spy continuously for two hours, tried to break the world record for singing 'Ten Green Bottles Standing on a Wall', starting at '10,948,361 Green Bottles', then burped and armpit-farted through some of Natalie's favourite songs. Mr Mason had even joined in at one point, playing on a kazoo.

At last they were driving among high hills coloured purple by heather, and along the banks of

Loch Baldie, an expanse of deep, still water. The car pulled up at the entrance to Tartan Towers Holiday Park. A huge tartan banner stretched above the gates, proclaiming:

'*Welcome to Saltimuchty –*
Home of the Loch Baldie
Beastie!'

'Beastie?' said Natalie
anxiously.

'Don't worry,' said
Matthew's mum. 'It's
just a silly legend.'

As everybody
climbed out of the
car, a large ginger-
bearded man strode
towards them. He wore
a swirling kilt, floppy hat,
long tartan socks and
an enormous sporran
that reached from his waist to just below his knees.
Across his T-shirt were emblazoned the words,
'*Tartan Towers – as much fun as you can have in*
a kilt!'

'Welcome! Welcome!' he called.

'Topaz MacTavish is ma name,
And havin' a hoot is ma game.
Have fun, relax, enjoy the facilities,
They're specially designed for all abilities!'

Matthew's dad shook the man's hand. 'Hello, Mr MacTavish. I'm David Mason . . .'

'Ahh! You're the man who is supposed ta
Mend ma broken rollercoaster!'

Mr Mason glanced nervously at his wife.

'Er . . . yes . . . that's what you asked me here
    to do . . .
But first I need . . . a tub of glue.'

Topaz MacTavish roared with delight.

'There's nae need tae talk in rhyme:
Even *I* don't do it all the time!'

He leaned closer to Matthew's dad. 'There's another ride gone on the blink yesterday – will ye mend that one too?'

Mr MacTavish grinned at the boys. 'I need ma park in tip-top condition if I'm going tae beat Bladderpool Pleasure Dome in the Fun Park o' the Year Award!'

'They've won it for five years in a row,' commented Danny.

'Aye, but not this time! Ma BoneShaker ride'll give us the edge *this* year.'

Mr MacTavish pulled an envelope from his gigantic sporran and Danny recognized the familiar logo of the Great Big Book of World Records on the front. 'Now, it's ma guess that one o' ye two bonny laddies is Master Danny Baker.'

Danny Baker
Tartan Towers Holiday Park
Saltimuchty
Scotland

'That's me!' said Danny.

'This letter arrived for ye this morning.'

Mr MacTavish reached into his sporran once more, pulled out some shortbread biscuits and handed one to each of his guests. 'Fare ye well! And beware the mighty wee midges – they'll give ye a nasty nip!' he cried, striding off to greet another carful of new arrivals.

The Silly Suitcase

The Great Big Book
of World Records
London

ARE YOU A RECORD
BREAKER?

Dear Danny

I have some good news and some bad news
regarding your attempt on the Alphabetically
Coordinated Suitcase-packing World Travel world
record. The good news is that all the items on
your list obey the rules (including the plastic
spider!). The bad news is that you must visit
the countries in alphabetical order, starting
with a town and country beginning with 'A'.
Saltimuchty in Scotland would have to be your
nineteenth trip, not your first.

The current record holder is Olaf Tufte of Mo in Norway, who set out to 'travel the alphabet' as many times as he could. He was on his fourth lap of the alphabet when he caught Yellow Fever in Yarim in Yemen, from a mosquito packed by mistake in Mopti in Mali.

These days, Olaf never leaves home, eating only alphabet soup and travelling alphabetically from room to room: bathroom, bedroom, dining room, hallway, kitchen, living room, then back to the bathroom to start all over again.

Enjoy your stay in Saltimuchty, Danny, and mind the Loch Baldie Beastie doesn't get you!

Best wishes
Eric Bibby
Keeper of the Records

Natalie and Mrs Mason were in the caravan, unpacking.

'Danny!' shouted his sister. 'What's going on in your suitcase?'

'Uh-oh.'

'What do you need a sombrero for?' asked Natalie, holding up the big straw hat. 'We're in Scotland, not Spain!'

'Why have you brought a sprout?' asked Mrs Mason, picking one out of Danny's case. 'And a sieve?'

'And a spanner?'

'And a set square?'

'And why bring the saddle off your old bike?' Natalie dangled a snail shell in front of Danny's eyes. 'This has to be the most useless piece of packing ever!'

'I was starting my attempt on the Alphabetically Coordinated Suitcase-packing World Travel world record,' Danny explained. 'We're in Saltimuchty in Scotland, so I had to pack things that start with the letter "S".'

Natalie took a bright-red tartan kilt from Danny's case. '*Kilt* begins with "K",' she told him.

'It's *Stewart* tartan,' answered Danny, and made a face to say, 'So there.'

Natalie began to pull more things out. '*One* sock, *one* slipper . . .'

'*One* skate . . .' said Mrs Mason, laughing. '*One* sporran . . .'

'The rules say you can only take one of anything,' said Danny.

'Then why *half* a pair of shorts?'

Natalie snorted. 'Because he's only got half a brain!'

Danny ignored her. 'I thought a *pair* of shorts would count as two things, so I cut off one leg.'

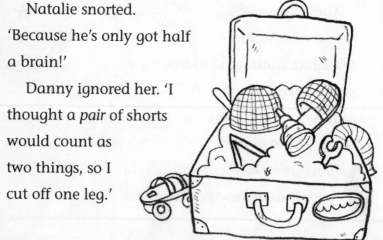

Matthew's mum rolled
her eyes and laughed.
'Well, Danny, you're going
to have to make do with
what you've brought.'

She picked up a can of
insect-repellent. 'It's spray-
time!' she announced.

'Urghh!' moaned Natalie as the fine mist of
chemicals covered her from head to foot. 'It stinks!'

'No worse than you,' said Danny.

'It's better than getting eaten alive by "mighty
wee midges",' said Matthew's mum, spraying the
boys too.

Danny put the slipper on his left foot, the skate

on his right foot, buckled
the kilt around his waist,
strapped on his sporran,
grabbed his case and
clomped out of the
caravan with Matthew.
Two tents stood nearby, one

a dull olive-green colour, the other shocking pink with big purple flowers printed all over it.

Matthew pulled a face. 'I hope no one thinks this is *our* tent.'

Danny nudged his friend. 'Let's have a quick peek inside.'

They gazed in wonder into Natalie's tent. Her fluffy pink sleeping bag lay on an air bed in the centre, with her fluffy pink slippers on top. A vase of freshly picked wild flowers and a pink vanity mirror stood on a small folding table in one corner.

Her make-up, lotions and jewellery were carefully arranged on a table in the other corner, along with a travel clock. She had stuck pictures of her favourite boy band, Boy$!!!, all over the inside of her tent, and placed magazines and books in the pockets beside the door. Nine pairs of shoes were dotted around the tent, while Matthew counted twenty-eight assorted shirts and tops draped over hangers along one side.

'When did your sister become Nat the Neat?' asked Matthew.

'It's because she's thirteen soon,' explained Danny. 'She says "grown-ups" like her are always tidy!' He rummaged around inside his suitcase. 'She should be careful leaving her shoes out like that,' he grinned, dropping the small plastic spider into one of Natalie's slippers. 'Creepy crawlies might get in.'

The boys slung their bags and clothes into their own tent and started unpacking. A moment later, Natalie stuck her head through the tent-flap.

'You forgot your sombrero,' she said, hurling the hat at Danny. She saw the mess of bags, comics, snacks and clothes piled up around the boys. 'Urghh! It looks like you've brought half your disgusting bedroom with you.'

Danny shrugged. 'Yeah, and Matt's brought half his! So what?'

'It's like a rat's nest,' said Natalie, wrinkling her nose. 'It stinks of . . . boys. I'm off!'

Danny and Matthew waited. A few moments later they heard a blood-curdling scream from Natalie's tent.

Danny grinned. 'Sounds like Nat just put her slippers on – *run*!'

At the far end of the funfair they could see The BoneShaker silhouetted against the late-afternoon sky. The boys headed towards it, pushing through queues of happy holidaymakers munching on hot dogs and candyfloss, waiting to ride the Bash-em-

up Dodgems and the Highland
Horror Ghost Train.

Matthew unfolded a map
of the park and consulted it
carefully.

'We need to go left here at the
Fling-a-haggis Stand,' he said.

They hurried past the
Swinging Sporran Crazy-
golf Course and resisted
the sweet, yummy smell
of cakes wafting from
the Witch's Cauldron

Cafe. Two minutes later the boys stood before
the rollercoaster, gaping at the black metal track
rearing up into the sky above them like a huge,
twisting, coiling snake.

'Ace,' breathed Danny.

'Cool,' agreed Matthew. 'I hope my dad gets it
fixed soon. I can't wait to ride *that*!'

'Me too. I'll be halfway through the TerrorCoaster
Grand Slam if I beat this one! Come on, let's check

out the pedal boats before it gets dark.'

Just as they reached the loch, a high wailing cry echoed eerily in the hills around them.

'What was *that*?' asked Matthew.

'I don't know,' replied Danny. 'Let's go and see.'

A path led them to a large wooden boathouse set back from the water's edge. The banner flapping outside read 'The Beastie Boat Hire', but the door was closed and heavily padlocked. A sign warned, 'Danger! Keep Oot!'

Topaz MacTavish was standing on the end of a

short jetty, gazing out across the dark water of the loch.

'Hello, Mr MacTavish,' said Danny. 'Did you hear a weird noise just now?'

'Was it a forlorn wail, like the wind howling across a desolate moor?'

The boys paused, then nodded.

'That was the Beastie!'

Matthew glanced at Danny and pulled a face. 'My mum says the Beastie's just a legend.'

Mr MacTavish shook his head. 'It's nae legend, laddie. It's a terrible monster o' the deep, with glowing red eyes and fangs like carving knives. Och, there's been many a sighting! Only last week six bonny sheep went missing, dragged down intae the cold, black water of the loch and *devoured*.'

Topaz MacTavish fixed them with his beady blue eyes.

'Beware! Take care!
It would nae be fair
If he gobbled up ye pesky pair!'

He leaned close to the boys and lowered his voice. 'Take ma advice: zip yer tent up tight and stay in yer beds. The Beastie's back and he's hungry . . . Now *scram!*'

In the middle of the night, Danny woke with a start. Matthew was shaking him urgently.

'Listen!' whispered his friend.

Danny listened and heard once again the eerie howling cry of the Beastie.

He caught his breath. 'Spooky! Let's wake Natalie up and see if she can hear it.'

The boys grabbed their torches and scrambled out of the tent. Just then another high wailing screech sliced through the still night air.

'Nats!' hissed Danny, unzipping the door of her tent.

Natalie struggled to wake up. 'Danny?' she said sleepily. 'What's the matter?'

'The Loch Baldie Beastie's coming!' he replied, shining his torch at her.

'I don't think so. *You're* the only monster around here!' she mumbled, pulling her sleeping bag over her head.

Danny and Matthew retreated to their tent.

'Did you zip Natalie's door up again?' asked Matthew.

'No, I forgot,' replied Danny. 'But she'll be fine. The Beastie won't eat her. She's poisonous!'

A Munch of Midges

Tartan Towers Holiday Park
Saltimuchty
Scotland

Dear Mr Bibby

Natalie's not happy. I left
her tent open last night and
when she woke up this morning
there were about fourteen
bigatrigtrillion midges swirling
around like smoke inside her tent.

midges

Nats fell asleep with her face and left arm
sticking out of her sleeping bag, and it looked
like every single bug in Scotland had taken a
bite. To make her feel better about it, I told

her that so many midge bites might be a world record, and Matt offered to count all the tiny red spots. She sort of said 'No', and a few other things too that I can't repeat. When she threatened to turn us into Beastie Burgers and Human Haggises, we scarpered.

We counted the bites anyway when she fell asleep in the caravan this afternoon. There were 3,457. Has Natalie broken the world record for being Munched by Midges?

3,457 bites

Best wishes
Danny Baker

The Great Big Book
of World Records
London

ARE YOU A RECORD
BREAKER ?

Dear Danny

Poor Natalie! She hasn't broken the record, but
she might be glad of that. Tell her the story
of Alfonso Bilious, who ran Cirque du Midge,
the world's one and only dancing-midge troupe.
Their beautiful mid-air ballet was a mesmerizing
sight, as the dark, billowing cloud of insects
ebbed and flowed, whirled and swirled, and
curled and twirled in time to graceful music.
Alfonso – 'The Midge Master' – stood beneath
them, dressed only in a pair of gold sequinned
shorts, conducting their movements with great
sweeping gestures, jumps and pirouettes.

Then, in Tegucigalpa, Honduras, on the last
night of their 1971 world tour, something went
horribly wrong. At the climax of the show, and

36

for no reason known to man or midge, the swarm
mysteriously turned on Alfonso, plummeting
from the sky like a thick grey blanket and
smothering him completely. The audience thought
this was part of the act and did nothing, until
eventually the midge-cloud drifted away into
the balmy evening air, where they were gobbled
up by a huge swoop of swallows.

By then it was too late for The Midge Master.
He lay dead on the ground, mangled by his
midges. Not one square micrometre of his body
was left un-nibbled. Doctors counted 13,555,889
separate bites.

So slap on the insect-repellent, Danny, and
don't mess with those midges. Enjoy the rest of
your stay at Tartan Towers!

Best wishes
Eric Bibby
Keeper of the Records

'When's The BoneShaker going to be mended, Dad?' asked Matthew.

Mr Mason stood at the small washbasin in the caravan, scrubbing the oil from his hands. He sucked in his breath and shook his head. 'Not until tonight, at the earliest,' he replied. 'The forward traction-sprocket has jammed, and that's put strain on the twizzle-bearing sprott-noggin accelerator.'

'So the bob-lobber won't engage with the flobble-flange,' said Matthew.

'That's right, and the brake's wedged in stop position.'

'Is that bad?' asked Danny.

'Very bad,' admitted Mr Mason. 'But don't worry, I can fix it.' He rubbed his hands dry. 'Have you two had breakfast?'

'Yeah,' answered Matthew. 'We're just going to play crazy golf.'

Matthew yawned as the boys headed out of the camping area and through the park. 'I heard that spooky sound again last night.'

'You should have woken me up,' said Danny, gliding along on his single roller skate.

Matthew shrugged. 'Mum's right. There's no such thing as the Loch Baldie Beastie. It was probably just an owl.'

The Swinging Sporran Crazy-golf Course was their favourite thing in the whole park. Instead of golf balls, Danny and Matthew had to knock mini haggises over the 'Snow-bound Muchty Mountains' on the first hole, through the 'Foaming River Spew' on the second, and into the mouth of a larger-than-life-size statue of Topaz MacTavish on the third.

To Danny's delight, when he successfully hit the target, the haggis rattled and gurgled down through the statue's body, then dropped out from under the owner's kilt with a satisfying plop.

They had to cross the 'Fifth Bridge' on the fourth hole, avoiding the toy steam train that crossed it twice every minute. As they approached the next hole, the 'Tartan Terror', Danny gasped and pointed down the course.

There was a huge, muddy three-toed footprint about five metres in front of him. The long thin claws on each toe had ripped the fabric of the tartan turf.

'That's not a legend,' said Matthew. 'That's real. It *was* the Beastie I heard last night!'

'You never

know, Matt,' said Danny. 'There could be a really big chicken on the loose!'

'Do ye *still* think it's a legend?' shouted Topaz MacTavish as he walked by on the other side of the fence. 'I'm going tae put some bait oot tonight, tae see if I can tempt it oot o' the water once more.'

'Why don't you use my sister, Natalie?' laughed Danny. 'She's a big worm!'

All day the park was buzzing with excitement about the monster footprint.

'Let's climb up to that tower on the hill behind the boathouse,' suggested Danny. 'If the Beastie pops out of the loch again, we'll get a good view from up there.'

As they reached the square stone tower, Matthew spotted a shiny brass plaque. 'Hey, Dan, look at this. It's a certificate from Mr Bibby!'

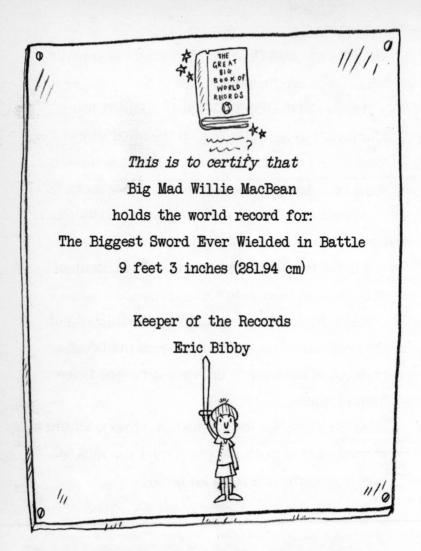

This is to certify that

Big Mad Willie MacBean

holds the world record for:

The Biggest Sword Ever Wielded in Battle

9 feet 3 inches (281.94 cm)

Keeper of the Records

Eric Bibby

The boys examined the huge broadsword displayed on the front of the tower, and read the story on the plaque beneath it.

'The Sword That Saved the Day'

The Battle of the Spew

1 April 1303

The English invaders were winning the battle, when gigantic Big Mad Willie MacBean, arriving late on to the field (because his breakfast porridge had been too hot to eat straight away) let out the terrifying MacBean battle-cry: 'AWAH WI' YER HEED!'

He charged into the lines of English soldiers, chopping off heads with great swipes of his massive sword. The English army turned and ran away. Only Edward, Earl of Nuttingham, stood his ground, and it was on this very spot that Big Mad Willie cut him in two, right down the middle, with one mighty blow from the sword.

The dark stains on the handle are said to be the dried blood of the earl.

The slain English soldiers were buried beneath this mound and the tower built on top of them. It is said that on the anniversary of the battle, when the moon is full, ghostly bodies rise up and wander the forest in search of their missing heads.

The boys stared down at the ground beneath their feet.

'Gross!' said Danny.

'Giga-gross!' agreed Matthew.

Just then, the spine-tingling wail of the Loch Baldie Beastie shattered the quiet of the forest.

'What shall we do?' whispered Matthew.

Danny took a deep breath and made a decision. 'I'm going down to the loch to investigate. If there *is* a Beastie, I want to see it.' He looked at Matthew. 'Are you coming?'

His friend nodded.

'Let's do it.'

The boys headed down the hill, creeping from tree to tree, until they were just a few metres from the boathouse. Suddenly, from inside the building, a loud unearthly shriek tore the air, followed by the bleating of terrified sheep.

The door swung open and a fearsome yellow head, a pair of blazing red eyes and a long green neck emerged into the dim light of dusk.

The boys gasped.

The creature lumbered out of the building. Its neck curved into two knobbly green humps on its back, followed by a thin swishing tail.

'Look!' said Danny.

Sticking out from beneath each hump were two skinny human legs, wearing stripy swim shorts and bright-blue flippers.

The Beastie's head bashed into a tree.

'Careful, Andy,' said a voice which seemed to come from the Beastie's bottom. 'Mr MacTavish won't be happy if you break his monster.'

'Aye, Ewan,' replied another voice. 'And he'll be

furious with *you* for trampling on the bagpipes and making them wail!'

'It was an accident! Now shut up and watch where you're going.'

They trundled down to the water and the Beastie paddled out into the loch.

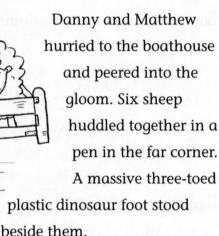

Danny and Matthew hurried to the boathouse and peered into the gloom. Six sheep huddled together in a pen in the far corner. A massive three-toed plastic dinosaur foot stood beside them.

'That's what made the footprint!' exclaimed Matthew.

'And that's where the Beastie's cry comes from!' said Danny, pointing to a set of bagpipes that lay on

the ground next to a microphone and an enormous loudspeaker. 'It's a hoax!'

'Should we tell?' asked Matthew.

Danny shrugged. 'I don't want to snitch,' he replied. 'But he *is* cheating.'

As the boys left the boathouse, they saw Topaz MacTavish heading towards them along the narrow path that skirted the loch.

'Quick!' said Danny. 'Back into the forest!'

In the nick of time, they scampered into the trees, but Danny had left two telltale footprints of his own in the dirt outside the boathouse: a slipper and a skate . . .

The BoneShaker

Danny and Matthew raced back towards The BoneShaker to find Mr Mason. Just as they got there, dazzling white floodlights snapped on all around the rollercoaster, illuminating it against the darkening sky.

Mr and Mrs Mason stood nearby with Natalie.

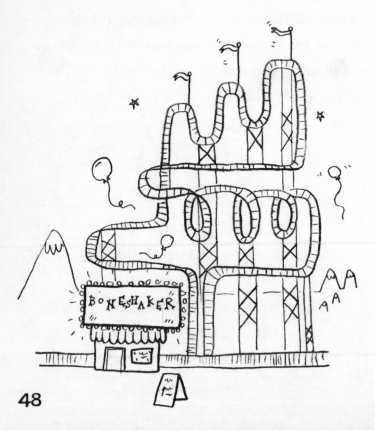

'Dad!' called Matthew. 'We've got something to tell you!'

'Later,' beamed Mr Mason. 'I've fixed The BoneShaker and we're going to have first go!'

'I'll stand here and watch,' said Matthew's mum. 'What about you, Natalie?'

'I'm not staying down here,' she replied. 'In case *they* decide to be sick up there!'

'Come on then!' cried Mr Mason, striding off towards the entrance gate.

'But, Dad . . .' said Matthew.

'Tell him later, Matt,' said Danny. 'I want to do the Wobble Walk and beat The BoneShaker!'

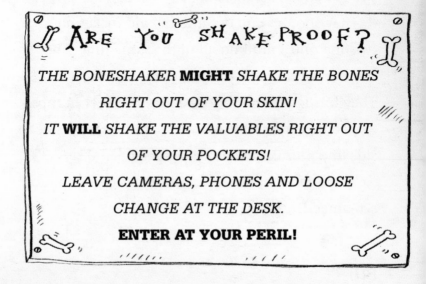

ARE YOU "SHAKE PROOF?"

THE BONESHAKER **MIGHT** SHAKE THE BONES
RIGHT OUT OF YOUR SKIN!

IT **WILL** SHAKE THE VALUABLES RIGHT OUT
OF YOUR POCKETS!

LEAVE CAMERAS, PHONES AND LOOSE
CHANGE AT THE DESK.

ENTER AT YOUR PERIL!

Word had spread quickly that The BoneShaker was mended, and as Danny, Matthew, Mr Mason and Natalie were strapped into their seats on the front two rows, they were joined by dozens of others in the seats behind.

BONESHAKER

The countdown began: 'Five . . . four . . . three . . . two . . . one . . . Shake off!'

They shot up and out into the air, rocketing, twisting and spiralling all at the same time. The roaring wind dragged at their hair and faces. They hurtled round sharp bends, flew over humps, zipped through tight corkscrews, rattled from side to side and plummeted down steep sudden drops.

'Aaaaaaaaaaaaaaaaaaaaaaaaaaaaaaaaaaaaace!' screamed Danny.

'Cooooooooooooooooooooooooooooooooooooool!'
bellowed Matthew.

They swooped around the final bend then shot
into a deep cavern in the earth, before screaming
back into the light on one huge backward loop.

As the rollercoaster reached the apex of the loop,
it slowed . . . creaked . . . and then stopped. The
riders were left dangling upside down, thirty-three
metres up in the air.

'Noooooooooooooooooooooooooooooooooooo!'
wailed Natalie.

Danny's kilt hung
down to his chin,
exposing his half-
pair of shorts. A
camera mounted
to one side of the
track flashed as it
took the photo.

'This is
supposed
to happen,'

explained Matthew's dad. 'Any moment, the brakes will release, the turbo-thrust zap-booster will kick in, and we'll rocket down to the finish.'

The boys held their breath, waiting for the last thrilling, spiralling descent to begin.

Nothing happened.

'Here it comes,' said Matthew's dad.

Nothing happened.

'Any second now . . .'

Nothing happened.

'Don't worry!' shouted Mr Mason to everyone on the ride. 'I think the trammel-dongler must have wedged against the Grot and Gubbins fluctuation-flap and locked the automatic brakes. Someone just needs to press the emergency brake-release button.'

'But you're the only person who knows that,' said Matthew. 'It could take hours for the people on the ground to work it out!'

'Um . . . oh yes. Er . . . lovely view isn't it?' said Mr Mason.

'It would be if it wasn't upside down!' whimpered Natalie, her face turning as pink as her knickers.

Danny saw people rushing around below and Matthew's mum staring anxiously up at them. Topaz MacTavish came out of a door at the base of the rollercoaster, then scuttled away.  Strange, thought Danny. He's not wearing his sporran.

The wind whistled gently through the steel track, carrying the laughing 'Caw! Caw!' of the rooks flying home to roost for the night. Below, a fire engine arrived and Danny saw the yellow hats of the firemen moving to and fro. They extended a ladder towards the riders, but it wasn't long enough.

'Look!' said Matthew. 'There's the boathouse where we saw the fake foot and the men in the monster suit.'

Danny looked where his friend was pointing. 'Yeah, and there's Mr MacTavish going inside!'

Soon orange flames and thick black smoke rose up from the boathouse.

'What's going on?' wondered Matthew.

Before Danny could answer, the rollercoaster juddered, fell a few metres and ground to a jarring stop again.

There were screams and a small boy just behind Danny said, 'I'm scared.'

'I want to get off!' cried another.

'I think we could be up here for a very long time,' whispered Mr Mason. 'We need to keep everybody's spirits up.'

Danny glanced at Matthew. 'We'll go and investigate what Mr MacTavish is up to tomorrow. Now it's time for a sing-song!'

'One man went to mow,' began Danny, 'went to mow a meadow. One man and his dog, went to mow a meadow!'

'Mrs M!' screamed Natalie to Matthew's mum far below. 'Tell him!'

Matthew took up the song. 'One man went to mow, went to mow a meadow. One man and his dog and a bottle of pop, went to mow a meadow!'

Matthew's dad joined in. 'One man went to mow,

went to mow a meadow. One man and his dog and a bottle of pop and a sausage roll, went to mow a meadow!'

The small boy behind Danny laughed and sang out, 'One man went to mow, went to mow a meadow. One man and his dog and a bottle of pop and a sausage roll and a sweaty sock, went to mow a meadow!'

Somebody else took over. 'One man went to mow . . .'

'Keep it going!' shouted Danny. 'Let's see if we can break the world record for "One Man Went to Mow" Singing on a Rollercoaster.'

The song went on and on:

'. . . and a can of worms and a treacle pud . . .'

Each person on the ride added their own silly item to the list, while Matthew kept a tally.

Meanwhile, from The BoneShaker's new position, Mr Mason had spotted a big red button set on to a panel on the ground directly below them. 'Look! That's the emergency brake-release button. If we could throw something at it and hit it hard enough, we'll be free!'

'. . . and a wooden leg and an oily rag . . .'

'But there's nothing to throw,' complained Matthew. 'We had to leave everything behind.'

'I kept a few things safe in my sporran,' said Danny. 'But I'm not chucking anything yet. We need to give the record attempt our best shot.' He turned to the others. 'Keep singing!'

'. . . and a bag of chips and a teddy bear and a bar of soap . . .'

Eventually the song came back round to Danny and he added a forty-sixth item to the list.

'. . . and a spotty bum, went to mow a meadow!'

Everyone laughed except Natalie, whose face by now had gone from pink to red to purple.

'I think Nat's nut's going to explode,' said Matthew.

Danny realized it was time to take action. He carefully undid his sporran and rummaged inside. Pulling out a spoon, he took aim and flung it at the big red button.

Missed.

He pulled out a stapler and flung that.

Missed again.

He pulled out a spanner and flung it as hard as he could.

With a satisfying 'CLANG!' the spanner hit the button right in the middle.

Something hissed . . . something clicked . . . something banged. With a sudden lurch, The BoneShaker rattled and rolled in three tight, thrilling spiral loops towards the earth.

'Aaaaaaaaaaaaaaaaaaaaaaaaaaaaaaaaaaaaaaaaace!' screamed Danny.

'Cooooooooooooooooooooooooooooooooooooool!' bellowed Matthew.

'Bleuuuuuuuuuuuuuuuuuuuuuuuuuuuuuuuuugh!' barfed Natalie.

Danny Breaker—
Record Breaker

Dear Mr Bibby

Last night, forty-eight
people (including me, Natalie,
Matthew and his dad) got
stuck upside down on The
BoneShaker for sixty-three
and a half minutes.

Forty-seven of us sang 'One Man Went to Mow'.
(Natalie wouldn't join in.)

We added forty-six items to the song before
the rollercoaster started again. The whole thing
was filmed on a CCTV camera and I've sent a
copy of the video as proof.

Did we break the record for Singing 'One Man Went to Mow' on a Rollercoaster?

I went back this morning and beat The BoneShaker! Now I've got a Certificate of Steadiness to prove I rode the rollercoaster, managed to stand up afterwards and do the Wobble Walk for the whole ten metres down the straight line!

Two down, two to go! Now for The BarfMaker!

Best wishes
Danny Baker

The Great Big Book
of World Records
London

Dear Danny

I'm sorry to tell you that you *haven't* broken
the world record for Rollercoaster-riding 'One
Man Went to Mow' Item-listing. On the very
same day as your attempt, fifty-three old-age
pensioners from Belper in Derbyshire claimed
the record on The SkullScrambler at Foulmouth
Abbey Theme Park in Devon. (Included in their
list of items were: a hot-water bottle, a pair of
false teeth and a Zimmer frame!)

However, the pensioners were the right way up!
Once again, Danny, you *have* set a new world
record, this time for Rollercoaster-riding
Upside-down 'One Man Went to Mow' Item-listing.
Congratulations!

60

I have enclosed certificates for you, Matthew and his dad. Anyone else who took part may claim their certificates from me.

I now look forward to your milkshake staying down on The Ballynoggin BarfMaker and your pants remaining dry on The Pontypyddl PantWetter!

Best wishes
Eric Bibby
Keeper of the Records

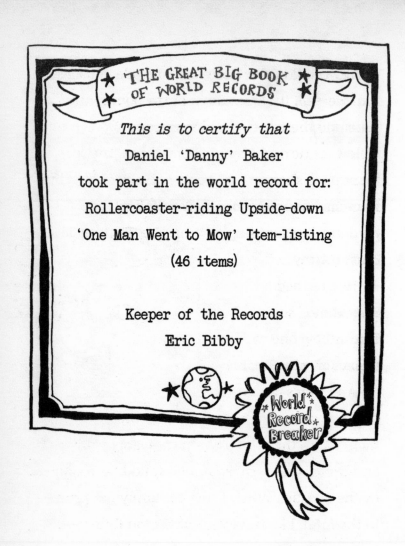

THE GREAT BIG BOOK OF WORLD RECORDS

This is to certify that
Daniel 'Danny' Baker
took part in the world record for:
Rollercoaster-riding Upside-down
'One Man Went to Mow' Item-listing
(46 items)

Keeper of the Records
Eric Bibby

World Record Breaker

Danny and Matthew stared at the pile of ashes
that were all that remained of the boathouse.
Here and there they could see scraps of green and
yellow fabric and a single big red eye. The six
kidnapped sheep
munched happily
on dandelions in the
grass nearby.

'He's burned
everything,' said
Danny. 'No one will
believe us now.'

'And that's fine with me,'
said Topaz MacTavish, striding towards
them along the path. His enormous sporran
was ripped and torn as though it had been gnawed
by the Beastie. 'When I saw yer funny footprints
in the mud, I knew ye'd rumbled ma little plot. I
jammed the brakes on The BoneShaker with ma
sporran tae keep ye two pesky kids oot o' the way
while I destroyed the evidence.'

'Why did you do it?' asked Danny.

'I was sick o' coming second tae Bladderpool in the Fun Park o' the Year Awards. I thought that bringing the Loch Baldie Beastie back tae life might swing it ma way.'

'But that's not fair!' exclaimed Matthew.

Mr MacTavish nodded thoughtfully. 'Aye, I know that now. I can see the error o' ma ways.'

'Anyway,' grinned Danny. 'Your park's a gigatintrillion times better than theirs. They don't have a gigantic sword that's chopped off heads! And The BoneShaker *rocks*! So . . .

Topaz MacTavish, stop your bleating.
You'll beat Bladderpool without *any* cheating!'

Mr MacTavish roared with laughter and reached into his sporran. He pulled out a crumpled newspaper and with a flourish unfolded it, holding up the front page for the boys to see.

'You're right there, laddie, I've been such a fool.
I'll leave the cheating tae Bladderpool!'

THE DAILY CLARION

Mythical unicorn sighted on Bladderpool Sands!
'The Loch Baldie Beastie's just a legend,' said Albert Dobb, Manager of the seaside town's Pleasure Dome. 'But The Bladderpool Unicorn is real!'

The Beastly
Bedroom

WARNING:
DON'T LOOK
UNDER THE
BED!

Icky Sticky Stuff

To the Keeper of the Records
The Great Big Book of World Records
London

Dear Mr Bibby

I'm making a 1:64 scale model of
last year's Penleydale Carnival
Parade for an art project at
school – out of earwax! My mates
on the football team have been giving me their
ear-goo for months and I've been keeping it
in a jam jar on my windowsill. I thought you'd
like to see a photo
of the model. If you
look closely, you can
see the 159 spectators

jam

earwax!

(including my mum and dad) and all the
miniature earwax floats I've made so far:

Pigling's Pit Wicked-witch Museum
The Greased Lightning Racing-badger Stables
Wyz Byz Supermarket's Five-a-day Custard-pie-
    eating Campaign
Penleydale Police Formation Pogoing Team
and . . .
The Dangly Dale Home for Disgruntled
    Dachshunds

Yesterday, my sister, Natalie,
was rummaging around in
my room looking for her
woolly blue scarf. I keep
the earwax model on top of
the wardrobe and she stuck her hand into it,
squashing the Lord Mayor and sixteen members
of the 9th Penleydale Girl Guide Troupe. She
wasn't happy.

Nat's hand

How big would my earwax model have to get
before it broke the world record?

Best wishes
Danny Baker

my earwax model ↑

Dear Danny

What a fantastic model! I'd leave the squished
Girl Guides as they are if I were you – they
add an interesting dramatic touch to the scene.

The Biggest Scale Model in Earwax of a Public
or Historical Event was an awesome creation.
In June 1978, 173 residents around Camel Hump,
Wyoming, USA, suffered a long and terrible
outbreak of Galloping Infectious Squirty-earwax
Disease. Local artist Mary Beth Baloney took
advantage of the situation and collected 3,198
litres of the icky-sticky orange stuff. That's
an average of 18.485 litres per person! She made
a 1:51 scale model of the famous Battle of the
Little Big Horn – otherwise known as Custer's
Last Stand – that eventually covered the entire

72

floor of her local basketball court.

Exactly one year after starting the project,
Mary Beth added Chief Sitting Bull and Chief
Crazy Horse to the scene and declared it
finished. Sadly, a week later, the model was
eaten by an infestation of ants, attracted by
the earwax's fruity odour.

So unless Galloping Infectious Squirty-earwax
Disease ravages Penleydale in the next few
weeks, it will take you a very long time to
break this record.

Best wishes
Eric Bibby
Keeper of the Records

Danny sat on the squashy beanbag by his bedroom window, unravelling the wool from an old blue bobble hat. Matthew perched next to him on a stack of *'It's a Save!' Goalkeepers' Monthly* magazines, carefully rolling the crinkly length of wool into a tight ball.

'Hey, I've had an idea for your tenth birthday party,' said Matthew. 'Why not have a party with everything in tens: ten mates, ten cakes, ten candles, ten games, ten party hats, ten sausage rolls . . .'

'Great idea, Matt!' exclaimed Danny. 'It'll be the Best Number-themed Birthday Party Ever! *And* it'll be boys only. No girls allowed, so . . . *no Nat!*'

'What about our mums? They'll need to be there, to do all the cooking and everything.'

Danny pondered for a moment. 'Well, they're not *actually* girls, so . . .'

Just then, Mum wandered into the room. The boys hastily hid the wool out of sight.

'Danny, where's your bed gone?' asked Mum, shaking her head in wonder.

Danny pointed to the far corner, where an enormous heap of clothes, a skateboard, a football, a sombrero, a velociraptor glove puppet, a green glow-in-the-dark skull and a bushy brown false beard were hemmed in by a bike, a dangerously crooked tower of *Yucky!* annuals for boys and a big straw donkey.

'It's under there somewhere,' he replied.

'This room's a tip,' said Mum. 'It needs—'

'Burning,' commented Natalie as she walked past the door.

Danny gazed around his bedroom. It was *always* messy, but because Mum had been so busy getting things ready for the new baby, she'd allowed him to let it get mega-messy.

From the ceiling hung a squadron of model aeroplanes, a flock of pterodactyls, a limp England flag and the entire solar system in papier mâché, minus Mars, because Danny had used it as a cricket ball. The walls were a collage of posters, along with two signed football shirts, four Walchester United scarves, three calendars and a clock. The wall opposite the window held all Danny's certificates from Mr Bibby.

The red carpet could only be seen as narrow, winding pathways around the islands of junk on the floor.

To get from the door to his wardrobe, Danny had to:

Squeeze between
  Smelly Sock Hill
  and Grubbypant
  Mountain . . .
Tiptoe through
  his eleven
  Guardians of Gorm
  action figures . . .
Roll a football out of the way,
and . . .
Leap over a loaded SplatterMaster gunge gun.

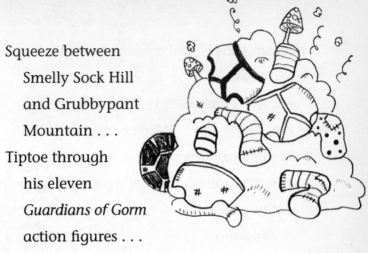

To get from the wardrobe to his chest of drawers, he
had to:
  Take a left turn at the dried cowpat (signed
    by Don Looney, United Kingdom Cowpat-
    balancing Champion) . . .
  Step over a pair of muddy trainers . . .
  Shuffle past the fish tank full of stick insects,
  and . . .
  Swerve round the stack of wombat-shaped
    jelly moulds.

To get from the chest of drawers to his bookcase,
Danny had to:

Bypass a stuffed armadillo . . .

Jump over the half-finished 1,000-piece
jigsaw of Creepy
Crawly Creek's
Slugs of the
World . . .

Tread on the
whoopee-
cushion
stepping stones,
and . . .

Climb over four large boxes
of lemon-puff
biscuits.

Danny's bookcase
was the only neat thing in the room.
Along the top two shelves, Matthew had
arranged all the storybooks in alphabetical order
by author, including Danny's favourites:

*Alien Poodles from Alpha Centauri Ate My
    Bottom!*
*Ziggy Watkins and the Invasion of the Vampire
    Robo-Spies*
and
Widdle and Poo and the Whiffy Blue Glue.

The shelves below these sagged under the weight
of all Danny's books of interesting facts, which
Matthew had organized by subject. Pride of place,
of course, was taken by *The Great Big Book of World
Records*, but there were also well-thumbed copies of:

What's That Bug?
What's That Smell?
and
*What's That Squashed
    Thing in the Road?*

The bottom shelf of the
bookcase held all twenty-six massive volumes of
The Encyclopedia of (Not Quite) All Knowledge.

Danny turned back to Mum. 'But my room's Ace!' he protested.

'Well, when you move into Natalie's room, I want it kept Ace *and* tidy,' said Mum. 'There must be *something* in here you can throw away.' She turned and pointed at a row of glass jars and bottles lined up on Danny's windowsill. 'And I don't want to see any of *that* yucky stuff once the new baby's here.'

The boys stood in silence until Mum had left the room, then Matthew gasped.

'You've not got to share a room with Nat the Neat, have you?'

'No way!' replied Danny. 'All that *girl-stuff*!' He mimed being sick. 'She's moving into the big spare room, I'm moving into her room and the new baby's going to sleep in here.' He shook his head. 'It's taken me ages to get it looking like this, and now I'm going to have to start again!'

Danny picked his way over to the window and gazed at the assorted jars and bottles that contained (among other things) dead daddy-long-

legs, elbow scabs, knee
scabs, apple pips,
snail-shells, bottle
tops, jumper
bobbles, chicken
wishbones, bits
of old snake skin,
dry seaweed, slugs'
eggs, Dad's belly-
button fluff, Grandad's
nose-hair clippings . . .

'You *can't* get rid of your collections!' said
Matthew.

'I'm not going to get rid of them,' replied Danny.
'Mum only said she didn't want to *see* them any
more.'

He looked around for a hiding place.

'Why don't *I* keep them just for now?' said
Matthew. 'I can count them all for you and make a
list. Then you could write and ask Mr Bibby if any
of them are record breakers.'

Danny put his hand on his friend's shoulder.

'Matt, you have got to be the Best Mate in the World Ever!'

Mum shouted up to them as she opened the front door. 'Boys, I'm just nipping out to buy a new fan belt for the car. Start tidying!'

'I'll tidy later,' grinned Danny. 'Let's get counting while the coast's clear.'

He grabbed his jam jar of toenails from the windowsill and the boys rushed downstairs. Matthew arranged the clippings in neat little piles of ten across the kitchen table, in long straight lines like soldiers on parade. He had just finished his calculations when Natalie strolled in carrying a ball of wool.

'Still knitting pink?' asked Danny.

'Yeah. Still knitting blue?' replied his sister. She peered closely at the little mounds on the table. 'What are those?'

'Toenails,' replied Matthew.

Natalie screwed up her face and gave a deep sniff of disgust. Unfortunately, she sniffed so hard that several of the smaller clippings shot straight up her nostrils.

'Urghhhhhhh!'

Her face became a wild-eyed mask of horror and panic. Her hands fluttered madly in the air. She gasped, and a huge, wet sneeze exploded from her nose, scattering the toenails far and wide across the kitchen floor.

'Nat!' cried Danny. 'It took me months to collect all those!'

His sister reached for a tissue and blew her nose. 'You'd better pick them all up, you horrible little monsters, or Mum'll go mad!'

She glowered like a princess looking down on her poor subjects, snatched up her knitting and flounced out of the kitchen.

'I think I'd better catalogue the rest of your collections at *my* house,' said Matthew.

Danny scanned the kitchen floor. 'It'll take ages to get all these toenails back in the jar – there's hundreds of them.'

'One thousand one hundred and eighty-seven, actually,' confirmed Matthew. He scratched his head thoughtfully, then pulled off his shoes and socks. 'Have you got any sticky tape?'

Danny smiled as he realized what Matt was suggesting. 'Yeah!'

The boys wrapped the tape around their feet, and began walking all over the kitchen, picking up the small, hard slivers of nail on their sticky soles. Their feet made pleasant farty-raspberry noises as the tape peeled off the tiles.

'I wonder if there's a record for Sticky-tape Gathering of Sneeze-propelled Toenail Clippings,' laughed Danny.

The Horrible Hoard - Part 1

Dear Mr Bibby

Matthew has started to make a list of all the bits and bobs I had in my jam-jar collection on the windowsill.

Yesterday he counted 1,187 toenail clippings, but we lost sixteen under the cooker and two up Natalie's nose!

Then he totted up the 296 coughed-up fur balls from my Auntie Sarah's cat, Babooshka. She's a Mongolian Rough-tongued Long-haired

furball

Mewler (the cat, not my Auntie Sarah) and spits one up every day. They've nearly filled the great big family-sized pickle jar I store them in. Some of the older ones are going a bit green and mouldy now.

I'm sure that there aren't enough fur balls to break a record yet, but could you tell me if I'm close? We've got more jars to sort through and if any of them do look like record breakers, I'll let you know.

Best wishes
Danny Baker

The Great Big Book
of World Records
London

Dear Danny

What an interesting start to your collection of
Bits and Bobs.

The Largest Number of Toenail Clippings
Collected from a Single Person's Feet is
3,273,771. The record is held by celebrity
grape-treader Vincenzo Piedatini, of Sicily. He
had an incurable fungus infection in his toes
that not only gave them a soft, grey, hairy
appearance, but also made his toenails extra
thick and horny. This condition, when combined
with regular immersion in grape juice, caused
his toenails to grow by over 9 cm a day. He had
to clip them morning, noon and night to keep
them under control, which is how he managed
to collect 3.67 tonnes of clippings during his

lifetime. Despite its revolting fungusy flavour,
the wine produced from Vincenzo's grape-
crushing sold for thousands of pounds a bottle,
as it was said to have miraculous healing
properties. It is *actually* the only known cure
for the St Columbus Collywobbles!

Your Collection of Fur balls from a Single
Cat record attempt shows a lot of promise. The
record stands at 1,572, but if Babooshka can
keep coughing up the balls, then there's no
reason why you won't break it in about four or
five years.

I can't wait to find out what other curious
Bits and Bobs you've got in your jam-jar
collection.

Best wishes
Eric Bibby
Keeper of the Records

Danny had been sleeping over at Matthew's house. The boys were on their way to play football and stopped at Danny's house so he could pick up his kit.

He dashed upstairs and into his bedroom.

The room was empty.

'Matt!' he yelled. 'My stuff! It's gone!'

In moments, Matthew joined him. 'Junk burglars!' he cried. 'Have they taken Nat's stuff too?'

Danny hurried into his sister's bedroom. Natalie's things *had* gone, but Danny's were there instead!

His bed was underneath the window, his wardrobe stood in the far corner and his bookcase against the wall next to it. In the middle of the room, a huge mountain of jumble rose almost to the ceiling. Teetering dangerously on top of it all was Danny's earwax model of the Penleydale Carnival Parade.

'They shifted it all while I was out!'

'Sneaky!'

Worst of all, Dad had not redecorated, and the walls, ceiling and carpet were still . . . PINK!

'Giga-gross!' said Danny.

'Biggagigga-gross!' agreed Matthew.

Mum and Dad appeared at the door.

'What do you think, Danny?' asked Dad.

'It's *pink*!'

'Sorry, but we need to clean and decorate the baby's room first. You'll have to put up with it for a while.'

'Why couldn't the baby have *this* room?'

Dad ruffled Danny's hair. 'Because your old room's next to ours, and if the baby starts crying in the night it'll be easier for us to get up and sort everything out.'

Mum walked over to the Trash Mountain and picked up a big bar of greasy yellow soap that was covered in squashed fleas. 'What is *this*?'

'It's my attempt at the record for
Collecting the Most Dog Fleas on
a Bar of Soap,' explained Danny.
'Those are from Buster, next door. I
was planning to go down to Dangly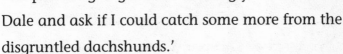
Dale and ask if I could catch some more from the
disgruntled dachshunds.'

'This is the kind of thing I don't want to see any
more,' said Mum, handing the soap to Danny.

'Yes, Mum,' he replied, quietly slipping the bar
of soap to Matthew when nobody was looking.
Matthew hid it in his trouser pocket.

'This room's *much* bigger than your old one,' said
Dad.

Yeah, thought Danny. I could fit a *humongous*
earwax model in here!

'I'll start to tidy up later, after the match,' he
promised, digging his kitbag and football boots
from the Trash Mountain. 'We've got a really
crucial league game against the Pympple Poppers.'

*

As he sat in the noisy changing room waiting to go out for the start of the game, Danny got his knitting out. He was getting better and quicker and as he clicked and clacked away with his needles, the tiny blue mitten grew swiftly. He was so engrossed in what he was doing that he didn't notice how quiet the changing room had become.

He held the mitten up to admire his handiwork and noticed all his Coalclough Sparrows teammates gawping at him.

'What?' he asked.

'Not here, Danny,' whispered Matthew. '*Not* cool.'

Just then the referee called them all out on to the pitch.

'Don't forget your knitting, Dani-*elle*,' sneered Maradona Potts, Danny's rival and the team's reserve goalie.

The game did not go well.

'Goal!' cried the Poppers' striker as he headed the ball past Danny and into the net for the second time in the game. Coalclough were losing 2–1, and there were only five minutes left.

'What's the matter, Dan?' said Matthew.

'I don't know,' replied Danny. 'Too much on my mind.'

Matthew grabbed an equalizer with two minutes to go. The Pympple Poppers pressed forward to snatch the winner, but twice Danny was lucky: first, the striker hit the bar,

and then, with seconds to go, he shot wide.

Maradona Potts smirked at Danny as they plodded wearily into the changing rooms.

'I'd have saved both those goals, Baker,' he said. 'They were easy-peasy. I heard Coach say if you play like that again, he'll put me back in goal. You can stay on the touchline and *knit*.'

The Horrible Hoard - Part 2

Dear Mr Bibby

Matthew's been doing his stuff again, sorting through more of my jam jars. He shut himself in the downstairs toilet at his house and counted 23,366 paper circles from a hole punch! He sat in the toilet because he was worried that a gust of wind might blow all the circles away, and it was the only place he could think of where there definitely wouldn't be any wind.

23,366!

I told him a toilet was the only place I could think of where there definitely would be some wind!

Next, Matt went through all the wood shavings
I keep when I sharpen my pencil crayons. There
were 3,715 of them, mostly
green because of the huge
drawing of the 1932 World's
Biggest Bogey Battle I did for
my art project last year.

bogey
battle

Have I paper-punched and pencil-sharpened my
way to a world record?

Best wishes
Danny Baker

ARE YOU A RECORD
BREAKER ?

Dear Danny

I doubt you will ever break the record for
collecting 'chads': the name for those little
bits of waste paper left behind by a hole
punch.

For thirty-nine years, Miss Elsie Trotter, the
Deputy Spy Librarian at MI54, worked alone
in the Top-secret Document-destruction Room,
shredding memos and letters using a hole punch.

At 3.29 p.m. precisely, on 21 February 1977, the
floor of the room gave way under the weight
of 61,453,888 tiny paper circles: the Largest
Chad Mountain Ever Created by a Single Person.
Underneath, a grisly discovery was made: the
skeleton of Agent James Pond, otherwise known

as 0077, who was thought to have defected
to the 'Other Side' in 1969. In fact, he had
burrowed under the growing pile of chads to
recover the bits of a top-secret document about
exploding bananas, but had then suffocated.

The record holder for Manual Production of
Pencil Shavings fared no better than Agent
Pond. In 2006, vegetarian tree-hugger Emmental
Donders of Switzerland reduced 78,349 wooden
pencils to a pile of 855,449 individual shavings.
She stuck the curly slivers of wood all
over her body and stood in the middle of a
forest pretending to be a tree. Unfortunately,
Emmental was *so* convincing that a logger cut
her down, and she is now a designer coffee table
in pop-star Madinner's Los Angeles home.

Best wishes
Eric Bibby
Keeper of the Records

'Has anyone seen
that blue jumper
Natalie knitted
for me last
Christmas?'
shouted Dad from
the top of the stairs.

'No,' answered
Mum from the living room.
'I've lost my blue woolly hat and Natalie can't find
her blue scarf.'

'They must've got shoved in a bin liner when
we were moving things around,' said Dad. 'They'll
show up again.'

In Danny's new room, the boys looked guiltily
at each other, and then at the balls of blue wool
hidden underneath a heap of old Walchester United
programmes by the bed.

'How's the tidying up going?' asked Matthew.

'Mum's made a start,' answered Danny, pointing
at a small pile of junk his mum had set aside to be
thrown away.

Matthew reached into the pile and dug out a Walchester United mug that had once contained milk. Danny had left it under his bed months ago and forgotten it, and the mug was now a spreading, creeping mass of furry green and orange fungus.

'Your mum can't make you get rid of this,' said Matthew.

'I know,' replied Danny, shaking his head. 'What's the matter with her? It smells great!'

Dad shouted up the stairs. 'Danny! Matt! It's time to go!'

'Come on,' said Danny. 'Let's go and beat the Black Head Squeezers.'

'Dan?' said Matthew.

'What?'

'Don't take your knitting.'

Danny had a nightmare game. The Squeezers

scored FOUR goals past him! The Coalclough
Sparrows were out of the Penleydale Schools
Cup, the trophy Danny had helped them win so
spectacularly last season!

'You're useless, Baker!' sneered Maradona Potts.
'You'll definitely be out of the team now!'

Dad came into the changing room with Mr
Collinson, the Coalclough Coach. Danny sat on a
bench, staring glumly at his boots. The rest of the
Sparrows were getting changed in shocked silence.
Matthew sat nearby, not knowing
how to cheer up his friend.

'What's the matter, Danny?'
asked Dad.
'I've never
seen you play
so badly.'

'I couldn't
concentrate,
Dad. I've
got too
many things

to think about: my room, my birthday party, wondering if I'll get a new brother or *another* sister, and . . . now I've let the team down.'

Dad sat down on the bench beside him. 'I once let in *thirteen* goals in three games. Queens Pork Rovers put *six* past me. But I kept practising and I went the next seven games without conceding one!'

Danny looked up at Coach Collinson. 'Potts says you're going to drop me and put him in goal.'

Coach Collinson frowned. 'I never said that, Danny. You're going to be the Best Goalkeeper in the World Ever, and a couple of bad games aren't going to change that. You're staying in the team.'

Danny beamed at his dad and punched the air.

'Ace! Starting next week, I'm going to break my own Longest Time without

Letting in a Goal world record!' he said. 'No one'll score past me for at least . . .' He looked at Matthew.

'Fifty-two games, or three thousand one hundred and twenty-eight minutes,' said his friend.

Dad laughed and ruffled Danny's hair. 'Now get changed, you two,' he said. 'We've got balloons to blow up!'

Happy Birthday, Danny!

Danny finished pumping up another balloon and tied a knot in the end. He glanced at the clock on the mantelpiece. 'It's half past six in the morning!' he whispered to Matthew, who had been staying over. 'We've been up all night doing this!'

Matt clicked his counter. 'Only two more and we've done ten thousand!'

Danny looked around. 'Apart from Mum and Dad's room, Nat's room and this little corner of the living room, we've filled the whole house!'

'Hey, I've just realized,' said Matthew, blowing up balloon 9,999, 'it's tomorrow now! It's your birthday! How does it feel, being ten?'

Danny inflated the ten-thousandth balloon and yawned. 'Tiring!'

Just then, he heard Mum and Dad moving around in their bedroom upstairs, talking urgently. Their door opened and Mum squealed.

'Danny!' shouted Dad. 'The baby's coming early! I've got to get your mum to hospital and we can't even get out of the bedroom!'

'Uh-oh!' gasped Danny.

He flung open the living-room door and came face to face with a dense, tightly packed wall of balloons. One tumbled from the top of the pile and bounced gently off his head.

'Pop them all!' he cried.

The house resounded with the pop and bang of bursting balloons as Danny and Matthew went to

work with Danny's knitting needles, slowly making
a path along the hall to the front door. Upstairs,
Dad used a pin and began to clear the way along
the landing. The noise woke Natalie and she joined
in with *her* knitting needles.

'What's going on?' asked Dad when he
eventually met up with Danny in the sea of
balloons at the bottom of the stairs.

'I wanted ten-thousand balloons for my number-
themed birthday.'

'Well, I reckon we've got about ten minutes to get
Mum out of here.'

They all carried on popping
and gradually reduced the
balloons from a sea to a
lake to a river to a pond.
Eventually Mum was able to
wade through them towards
the front door, carrying a
small overnight bag.

'Matthew,' she
said, breathing

heavily, 'phone your mum. Tell her the baby'll be here very soon and I've got to get to the hospital. Ask her if she can come round right away.'

She turned to Natalie. 'You know where all the party things are. I'm leaving you in charge.'

'Don't worry, Mum,' Natalie replied sweetly. 'I'll take care of everything.'

Mum and Dad hurried to the car and drove away. Natalie watched them go, then a slow, menacing smile spread across her lips. 'Did you hear that, you two?' she growled. '*I'm* in charge!'

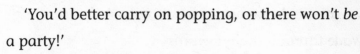

'There's not supposed to be any girls at my party,' said Danny. 'You'd better not mess it up.'

'You'd better carry on popping, or there won't *be* a party!'

'You're not the boss of me!'

'I am till Mum and Dad get back!'

Danny glared at his sister, said nothing and carried on popping.

By the time Matthew's mum arrived, the carpets were strewn with ten-thousand multicoloured strips of burst balloon.

'The first thing we need to do is clear up this lot,' she said. 'Then we can get everything ready.'

The party had to start at ten o'clock, and by the time Danny's friends began to arrive, the carpet was clear, the table was set and the games were prepared.

'Any word from the hospital, Mrs M?' asked Danny.

'Not yet,' replied Matthew's mum.

Natalie began giving orders, telling the guests where to leave their shoes, hang up their coats and put their presents. She told them to sit down, be quiet and keep still.

'This is like being at school,' said Harry Warburton.

'Who put you in charge?' asked Jack Dawkins.

'My mum did, so you have to do what I say,' insisted Natalie.

Tom O'Brian snorted. 'Why?'

'Because I'm thirteen now, and you're not!'

Soon eight of Danny's friends were there – only Sarwit Chudda hadn't turned up.

'We'll start without him,' said Natalie.

Danny frowned at Matthew. 'I hope he's going to come, or the whole "ten" thing doesn't work.'

The front doorbell rang.

'I bet that's him!'

Danny opened the door and gasped. It wasn't Sarwit, it was the postman. He peeped out from behind ten massive black sacks piled up on the doorstep.

'Ten-thousand birthday cards from the Walchester United Supporters' Club for Mr Danny Baker!' he announced.

'How did they know?' asked Danny.

'Dad arranged it,' said Natalie.

The postman handed Danny another letter. 'And

a Special Delivery from Number 10 Downing
Street . . . from the Prime Minister himself! Happy
birthday, young man!'

'And that was your mum's
idea,' said Mrs Mason.

'Mega-Ace!' laughed
Danny.

'Mega-cool!' agreed Matthew.

The nine boys shifted the heavy
sacks up to Danny's bedroom.

'Right,' said Natalie when they came back down.
'Time to play Musical Bumps.'

'Don't you mean Musical Trumps?'

'What?'

'It's the same game, but you have to sit down on
whoopee cushions.'

'Yeah!' chorused the other boys.

'After lunch, we're going to play Who's Got the
Loudest Trump?' said Danny. 'Matt's brought a
soundometer.'

'I think one trump-based game's enough,' said
his sister.

Danny grinned. '*Then* we're going to have a Treasure Hunt.'

'That sounds nicer.'

'Yeah, I'm calling it Follow Your Nose! Matt's been creating stinky stuff with his chemistry set. He's going to hide test tubes full of smelly goo around the house and we all have to find them!'

'How about Blind Man's Buff?' suggested Natalie.

'Don't you mean Blind Man's Armpit?'

'What?'

'Someone gets blindfolded,' explained Danny, 'then they have to sniff everyone's armpit and guess who they are!'

Natalie's nose wrinkled in disgust. 'I've had enough of this. I'm going to help Mrs Mason get the food ready.'

Danny heard the phone ring in the kitchen and raced in. 'Is it Mum? Is it Sarwit?'

'Sorry, Danny,' replied Matthew's mum. 'It was a wrong number. I'm sure we'll have some news soon.'

The boys began to play their games. Danny

was having fun, but he kept glancing out of the window, hoping to see Dad's car pull up or Sarwit skipping down the road.

Halfway through Stick the Spot on the Bott, Natalie came out of the kitchen carrying a plate of sausage rolls.

'Why can't you play Pin the Tail on the Donkey, like normal people?' she asked.

'Boring!' shouted Jimmy Sedgley, staggering around blindfolded and trying to place a small red sticker on a drawing of Thelma McCurdie's big pink bottom.

'Lunch is ready!' announced Mrs Mason.

'Yeah!' yelled the boys, pushing and shoving to get into the dining room.

The table was piled with food and in the centre stood Danny's ten-tiered chocolate cake, with ten red candles on top. Natalie had made little cards with each boy's name on and had placed them around the table showing them where to sit. These were scattered, as greedy hands began to snatch pies and pizzas.

Natalie scowled furiously as the boys ignored her seating plan and sat wherever they wanted.

Matthew's mum bustled in and out of the kitchen, filling cups with juice and dolloping jelly

into bowls. Finally
she lit the ten candles
on the cake and
Danny blew them out,
making a secret wish
as everyone sang 'Happy
Birthday to you'.

Just then the phone rang
in the kitchen again and Mrs
Mason went to answer it. Danny and Matthew
listened intently.

'Hello, Mrs Chudda . . . Oh no! Hot bottom . . .
cold nose . . . wobbly ear . . .
Parrot Pox!'

'Sounds like Sarwit's
definitely not
coming,' remarked
Matthew.

'The record
attempt's
scuppered!' said
Danny. 'Now all I need

is another sister and the rest of my *life*'s scuppered!'

'Hey, Dan!' shouted Sam Walters. 'Your dad's car just pulled up outside!'

'Is Mum with him?'

'Yeah, and she's carrying a bundle.'

'Is it blue?' asked Danny.

'Is it pink?' asked Natalie.

'It's white!'

Moments later the front door opened and Dad shouted, 'We're back!'

Danny and Natalie glared at each other, then rushed into the hall to see the new baby cradled in Mum's arms. It was swaddled in a soft white blanket and all that was visible was a round, red, wrinkly face.

'Is *he* a boy?' asked Danny.

'Is *she* a girl?' asked Natalie.

Everyone crowded round. Mum smiled and began slowly to unwrap the blanket.

Danny held his breath.

Suddenly the baby kicked the cover away and out popped a little foot wrapped in a tiny blue bootee.

'IT'S A BOY!' yelled Danny. 'My wish came true!'

He high-fived with Matt and all the boys cheered.

'Yes,' said Dad. 'And he's already got a terrific left foot!'

'Happy birthday, Danny!' said Mum.

Natalie shrugged, smiled and planted a big wet kiss on her new brother's cheek.

'What's his name?' she asked.

'Joseph,' replied Mum.

'Joe,' said Dad.

'Joey,' corrected Danny.

'Hey, Dan, your record attempt's back on,' said Matthew. 'Joey arriving means you've got ten boys at your party after all!'

'Oh yeah! And it's *his* birthday party too!' said Danny. 'Does he want a sausage roll?'

'I'm sure he will,' laughed Mum. 'But not for another two or three years!'

Much later, when the party was over and the guests had gone home, the family crowded into the baby's newly decorated room. Joey lay in his cot, waving his crinkly pink hands in front of his face as if he was batting away invisible flies.

Danny opened the door of a cupboard near his brother's cot and an avalanche of blue baby-sized thumbless mittens tumbled out on to the floor.

'Those are the same colour blue as my missing jumper!' exclaimed Dad.

'And my blue scarf!'

'And my blue hat!'

'I wanted to knit ten thousand of them, but I ran out of wool,' explained Danny.

'How many are there?' asked Mum.

'Three thousand, eight-hundred and fifty-nine,' he answered. 'So Matt says.'

'How many hands did you think he'd have?' laughed Dad.

Danny picked up two of the mittens and pulled them over his brother's hands.

'Happy birthday, Joey,' he said.

Danny Breaker - Record Breaker

Dear Mr Bibby

I am ten years old today and I've just had a birthday where everything was in tens — it even started at ten o'clock! I had ten boys at the party (including my new brother, Joey, who was born this morning!), we popped 10,000 balloons and played ten different games.

At lunchtime, we had:

Ten sausage rolls each

Ten pizza toppings

Ten flavours of ice cream

Ten flavours of juice

Ten flavours of crisps

Ten flavours of jelly

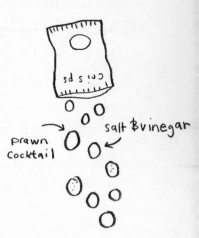

prawn cocktail

salt & vinegar

Ten tiers on the cake, with
Ten candles on top

I had ten presents:

A lump of ten-million-year-old
   fossilized sabre-toothed-tiger poo
   (From Matthew)
A number ten Walchester United
   shirt signed by our Brazilian
   striker, Tantrum
   (From Dad)
A 10,000-piece, ten-sided
   jigsaw of wiggling worms
   (From Mum)
Ten green bottles of
   flower-scented bath foam
   (From Natalie - ha ha, very funny!)
Ten Rotting Chowhabunga seeds
   (From Grandad Nobby)
Ten tins of baked beans
   (From Grandma Florrie)

Ten Wibberley Wobberley Jellies
   (From Sally Butterworth)
A ten-pin-bowling voucher
   (From Matthew's mum and dad)
A 10 kg bag of chocolate footballs
   (From the Coalclough Sparrows)
A gift-wrapped box of ten freshly coughed-
   up fur balls
   (From Auntie Sarah and Babooshka the
   cat)

furballs

I also got 10,000 birthday
cards from Walchester United
Supporters' Club and a card
from the Prime Minister at 10 Downing Street!
I've had the Best Number-themed Birthday
Ever, but was it a record breaker?

Best wishes
Danny Baker
(Aged ten exactly!)

The Great Big Book
of World Records
London

ARE YOU A RECORD
BREAKER?

Dear Danny

Happy birthday! I hope you had an 'Ace' party.
Your presents are fantastic. I have enclosed a
copy of *Mr Bibby's Little Book of Favourite
Records* as my birthday present to you. This
just so happens to be the tenth year it has
been published, and so fits perfectly with your
ten-themed birthday!

Unfortunately your attempt did not break
the record, which has stood for almost two
centuries. On 21 June 1821, Empress Hildegard
XXI of Bumstein Humbug reached the age of
twenty-one. To celebrate, she had a brand-new
palace built, with twenty-one flags flying from
its twenty-one turrets. There were twenty-one
rooms, twenty-one windows and twenty-one doors.

She had twenty-one portraits painted of herself
and hung one in each room.

She decided that every tree and flower in her
Empire should be uprooted, except for the ones
growing in her own twenty-one-acre garden.

Then she ordered that, from now on, only people
of her own age would be allowed to live in
Bumstein Humbug. Everyone above or below the
age of twenty-one was exiled to foreign lands.

Hildegard's Big Mistake was to decide that her
army would have only twenty-one soldiers. King
Alfred XXXXVII of Mangrovia saw his chance
and invaded Bumstein Humbug on the final day
of her Imperial Majesty's twenty-one-themed
birthday party, which had lasted for twenty-
one days. He thoughtfully sent 21,000 troops, in
order not to spoil the number-theme.

So although Hildegard recorded the Most

Complete Number-themed Birthday Ever, she was also dethroned and sentenced to spend the next twenty-one years of her life replacing all the trees and flowers she had destroyed.

As you can see, Danny, you would have to be at the very least a prince, and probably a king, to stand any chance of beating Hildegard's record. However, I *do* have some very good news for you.

This morning I received a letter from your mum, telling me that you have knitted 3,859 blue thumbless baby mittens for your new brother, and asking if this qualifies as a world record. I have searched our vast database and can find no previous claim for this amazing feat of patience, dedication and endurance. As I know from personal experience, knitting is not as easy as people think!

So once again you have *set* a new world record, this time for the Biggest Collection of Hand-knitted Unicolour Thumbless Mittens.

Your mum didn't know what she would do with
all those mittens, as the baby will only need
a couple of pairs. Might I suggest you donate
the ones Joey doesn't need to the Siberian
Bare-legged Husky Rescue Centre in Murmansk,
of which I am patron? These poor dogs have no
fur from the knees down, and thumbless mittens
would be ideal for keeping their paws warm! If
you send them to me, I will be delighted to take
them along on my next annual visit.

Well done, Danny! You have achieved another
stupendous record. Amazingly this is the tenth
certificate I have sent you, so not only have
you reached double figures in your age, but
also in your world records!

Best wishes
Eric Bibby
Keeper of the Records

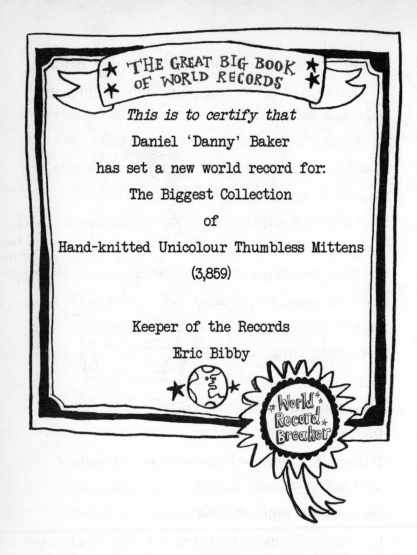

THE GREAT BIG BOOK OF WORLD RECORDS

This is to certify that
Daniel 'Danny' Baker
has set a new world record for:
The Biggest Collection
of
Hand-knitted Unicolour Thumbless Mittens
(3,859)

Keeper of the Records
Eric Bibby

World Record Breaker

Danny and Matthew were parcelling up 3,855 mittens, ready to send off to Mr Bibby for the bare-legged huskies in Murmansk. Mum sat nearby with

Natalie, who was holding Joey carefully in her lap.

Dad walked in carrying paint colour charts and wallpaper samples.

'Danny, what colour would you like your new room?' he asked.

'I don't want it decorated,' replied Danny. 'It's perfect as it is.'

'But it's pink!'

'Not any more!'

Except for the wall containing his certificates from Mr Bibby, Danny and Matthew had covered every inch of wall-space in birthday cards, overlapping each other like brightly coloured feathers. Danny's birthday presents and other junk were spread across the pink carpet. In the corner of the room, the boys had constructed a den like a huge black igloo out of the remaining card-stuffed mailbags. There wasn't

a centimetre of pink to be seen anywhere, and the only space left was the big dark space under Danny's bed. *That* was waiting for the Return of the Jam Jars.

'Are there any big bogeys in there?' asked Mum.

'No.'

'Any nitty soap?'

Danny shook his head. Not yet, he thought.

'Any disgusting creatures?'

'Only Danny and Matthew,' said Natalie.

At that moment, there was a burbly-bubbly, rumbly-raspy, gurgly-gushing sound from Joey's nappy.

Natalie's face crumpled as a stupendous stink wrapped around her and then drifted away into the room.

'Phwoar!' cried Danny. 'That's his niffiest nappy yet!'

'It's not as bad as your toxic toes, or your grandad's Rotting Chowhabunga,' said Matthew.

'Maybe not, but you'd better start making a whiffometer, Matt,' said Danny, holding his nose. 'We need to get measuring these pongs!'

Dad rescued Natalie, lifting Joey from her arms.

'All boys stink!' said Nat, fleeing the room.

Danny and Matthew followed Mum and Dad into Joey's room to watch the nappy being changed. Dad cleaned the baby up and Joey lay on his back happily kicking his feet at an imaginary football and still shaking his fists at imaginary flies.

'Are you happy with your baby brother?' asked Mum.

'Yeah! He knows how to get rid of Nasty Nat!'

'You don't get rid of me *that* easily!' said Natalie, pinching a wooden clothes peg on her nose as she marched into the bedroom to join the others at the foot of Joey's changing mat.

Suddenly Joey gave a little squeal, and a tall, thin tower of wee shot a metre in the air, curling gracefully up . . . and then down . . . straight on to the fluffy pink pompoms on his sister's fluffy pink slippers.

'Mum! Tell him!' cried Natalie, and fled the room for good.

'Ace!' cried Danny.

'Cool!' agreed Matthew.

Danny laughed. 'When you've finished making the whiffometer, Matt, you'd better make a *wee*ometer too! Joey's *definitely* going to be a record breaker, just like me!'

Turn the page to read an exclusive extract of

THE WORLD'S
LOUDEST ARMPIT FART

Out now!

WARNING!
SHE'S
BACK!

THE PENLEYDALE CLARION

Dirty Do-ings in Burly Bottoms!

By Reginald Heap, Chief News Reporter

An illegal Yorkshire cheese caused uproar last weekend at the finish of the Penleydale Junior Uphill Cheese-rolling Race.

For the 143rd year running, competitors pushed their regulation circular thirty centimetre Waxy Penleydale Cheeses along the traditional ten-kilometre course. The route took them up Boggart's Nose, across Miggin's Mop and over Hangman's Hump, before finally dropping down into Burly Bottoms.

With the finishing line in sight, the temperature hit a Penleydale record of 33.7°C. The lead cheese, being rolled by new-boy Maradona

'The Cheeseboy' Potts, disintegrated and melted, and roller after roller was sent tumbling on the greasy liquid cheese.

Ollie 'The Drainpipe' Snodgrass, age 11, of Hogton, kept his head – and his feet – and rolled his cheese over the pile of fallen competitors to win. Local boy Danny 'Record Breaker' Baker, who won last year's race in record time, broke a small bone in his foot, but hobbled on to finish in seventh place.

Judge Harry Clegg explained, 'The Waxy Penleydale is highly resistant to extreme temperatures, and would never melt like Maradona's cheese did. Closer inspection of the offending fromage confirmed that it was an illegal Grimsdyke Crumbly, disguised to look like a Waxy Penleydale. The Grimsdyke is lighter than the Penleydale, so it's easier to push uphill.'

Maradona Potts, now renamed 'The Cheatboy', was disqualified, and banned from competing in the race For Ever (+ ten years).

Result:

1st: Ollie 'The Drainpipe' Snodgrass

2nd: Trixibelle 'Bossyboots' Wolstenholme

3rd: Kristian 'The Bookworm' Renshaw

4th: Jack 'The Teabag' Spratt

5th: Samantha 'Tufty' Tompkins

6th: Matthew 'The Calculator' Mason

7th: Danny 'Record Breaker' Baker

8th: Ryan 'The Zombie' Wilkins

9th: Steve 'Snotbucket' Snitterton

10th: Carly 'Jam Butty' Benson

Retired hurt: Tommy 'Spiffy' Spofforth, Lucy 'Nose-picker' Knowles, Billy 'The Big Toe' Bowling

Disqualified: Maradona 'The Cheatboy' Potts

Hard Cheese

To the Keeper of the Records
The Great Big Book of World Records
London

Dear Mr Bibby

I've got a plaster cast up to my knee because
I hurt my foot when I slipped on a cheese. I'm
going to miss the start of the new football
season, and my doctor said I'll be out for four
weeks. My Grandad Nobby says I'm lucky it's only
four weeks. When he slipped on the
Rotting Chowhabunga seed-pod, he was
out for four decades!

my
leg

The doctor counted all the times
I've needed treatment because of my record
attempts, including:

My unwashed 207-spot bottom
My dangerously stinky feet
My walking-backwards-Wonderfluff-
   nappy-box-on-the-head incident
My boffin-baffling gobbledegook
My hospital-food-fuelled mighty trump
And my whistling, budgie-costumed, up-a-tree
   Spanish cramp.

(spotty
bum

When the doctor added these to all the
other times I've been with coughs, injections,
infections and stuff, I've had to see a doctor
seventy-nine times. She said that must be a
record. I *think* she was probably joking with me,
but *is* it a record?

Best wishes
Danny Baker

PS I only need to get through one more match
without anyone scoring against me, to break
the record for Most Consecutive Games without
Conceding a Goal. Keep your fingers crossed!

ARE YOU A RECORD
BREAKER ?

Dear Danny

Yes, I'm afraid the doctor *was* joking with you.
The record for Highest Number of Separate
Incidents Requiring Medical Treatment belongs
to Elmer Boggs of Picatinny, New Jersey, USA.

During his lifetime, Elmer broke every bone
in his body at least once, *including* the small
bones in both ears. He pulled every muscle, and
tore every tendon. Elmer was stung by jellyfish,
bees, wasps and a scorpion, and was bitten by
185 different kinds of animal, including a cow,
a squirrel, a bushbaby, a shark, a tortoise and
a ladybird. He also had 2,469 separate diseases
and made a total of 23,423 visits to the doctor.

Unwisely for someone who had such an accident-prone life, in 1984 Elmer volunteered to put his head in a lion's mouth to raise money for charity. This, of course, was a big mistake, and when the lion sneezed . . .

Recordologists cannot agree if his death should be included in the total, as he was seen by a doctor to pronounce him dead. I think it should, so I have.

Good luck with your first game back, Danny. I hope you manage to keep a clean sheet and break another record. I'll be keeping my fingers, toes, ears, legs *and* eyes crossed!

Best wishes
Eric Bibby
Keeper of the Records

Danny and his best friend, Matthew Mason, arrived at Walchester United for the first home game of the new season. The ground was full to bursting. The crowd had been waiting all summer for this, and excitement fizzed around the stands. Danny manoeuvred his plaster cast with some difficulty along the row of seats and sat down next to Matthew. The boys joined in the singing and chanting:

'Walchester United are the best team in the world!
After Barcelona, Real Madrid, AC Milan, Juventus,
    Man United and Chelsea!
Oh, and Bayern Munich, Ajax and all the teams in
    Brazil!
And Accrington Stanley, who beat us in the Cup
    two years ago!
Apart from that we're the best team in the world!'

The shrill blare of trumpets echoed through the stadium and the singing turned into a mighty roar. Danny and Matthew looked towards the tunnel,

just below where they sat, and saw
two men scurry on to the pitch
carrying a large circular sign
emblazoned with the words,
'Wibberley Wobberley – the
Jellies from Mobberley'.

Suddenly a huge red jelly
burst through the sign and wibbled
and wobbled out to the centre circle,
kicking a football and waving to the crowd.

'Let's give a big Walchester United welcome to
our new sponsors, Wibberley Wobberley Jellies,'
announced a voice over the loud speaker. 'And say
"Hello" to our new mascot, Wibbles the Dribbling
Jelly!'

Wibbles wore a red peaked cap, and the see-
through red plastic jelly costume ballooned out
from around his neck like a horrible bell-shaped
dress. His red hands stuck out from the side and his
skinny red legs from the bottom.

'I don't believe it,' groaned Danny.

'It's worse than Wally the Wall!' said Matthew.

'It's even worse than Gogo La Gamba, Real Marisco's pink prawn mascot. It doesn't even look like a jelly and you can see the man inside.'

Matthew peered closer. 'Isn't that Jack Dawkins's big brother? I thought he was training to be an astronaut.'

'Looks like he became a jelly instead!'

Just then another sound cut through the cheers of the crowd.

'Daaaaaaaannnnnnnnyyyyyyyyyyyyyyyyyy!'

The boys stared at each other in disbelief.

'It's not . . .'

'It *can't* be . . .'

'Hiiiiiiiiyyyyyyyyyyyyyyyyyaaaaaaaaaaaaaaaa!'

'It is!'

Five rows behind them, wearing a red Walchester United shirt, her bright-red hair twisted into two long pigtails and tied on the ends with ruby-red ribbons, was Sally Butterworth.

Danny cringed as he remembered his and Matthew's first meeting with Sally, in Spain just a few months before. Not only had she scored a goal against him in a game of beach-football, she had tricked him into winning his most embarrassing record of all: 18 minutes and 47 seconds of Budgie-costumed Perched-in-a-tree Kissing! Even worse, she had made him fall out with Matthew.

Sally waved furiously, then rolled her tongue and squinted. She edged along the row of seats and skipped down the stand towards them. Danny realized with horror that there was an empty seat beside him.

'Hiya!' beamed Sally. 'Remember me?'

'No, who are you?' replied Matthew.

Sally laughed, but her smile instantly turned to a look of concern as she noticed Danny's leg. 'What have you done?' she asked, sitting down in the vacant seat.

'Slipped on a cheese,' explained Danny.

'Is it broken?'

'What, my foot or the cheese?'

Sally punched Danny playfully, but hard, on the arm.

'Ow!' he complained. 'What're *you* doing here, Sally?'

'I'm with Wibberley Wobberley,' she said. 'My dad's the Regional Manager, so you'll be seeing a lot more of me from now on.'

'Your dad's a jelly salesman?' asked Matthew.

'Yeah! How cool is that?' Sally smiled at Danny and rested her hand on his. 'Do you like jelly, Danny?'

'Yeah . . .'

'I can get you as much jelly as you can eat.'

Suddenly Danny had an idea. He pulled his hand away and folded his arms.

'Could you get me enough jelly to break a record?' he asked.

'Course I can. Dad's got thousands of boxes full of "experimental" jelly-mixes that nobody wants.'

'*Experimental* jelly-mixes?'

Sally counted the different flavours on her fingers. 'Caviar and Custard.'

'Gross!'

'Turnip and Trifle.'

'Mega-gross!'

'Fig and Fish Finger.'

'Giga-gross!' said

Matthew.

Sally nodded. 'They made people throw up, and it was hard to get the mix right: they either wibbled too much or they didn't wobble at all. Anyway, you can have them all if you want.'

'Ace!' said Danny.

Matthew said nothing.

'*I* broke the County Junior Jelly-juggling record, with three balls of Pepperoni Pizza and Pomegranate jelly,' boasted Sally. 'Two minutes, fifteen point four seconds.'

Danny was impressed. 'You can juggle jellies?'

'Duh! If I couldn't juggle jellies, I wouldn't have broken the County Jelly-juggling record, would I?'

Matthew nudged Danny on the arm. 'Here come the teams.'

The trumpets blared once more and the Walchester United and Downmouth Albion players ran out on to the pitch in two long lines. The roar of the crowd wrapped around Danny, Matthew and Sally and pulled them to their feet to cheer.

'By the way,' shouted Sally as the players' names were announced. 'Have you seen who your school team is playing this season?'

'No,' replied Danny. 'Why?'

Sally didn't answer. She flashed Danny a huge smile, then turned back to watch the game.

'COME ON THE WIBBERLEY WOBBERLIES!' she screamed.

THE WORLD'S
BIGGEST BOGEY

STEVE HARTLEY

TO THE MANAGER
The Great Big Book
of World Records
London

Dear Sir,
I have been collecting
bogeys from my nose for the
last two years.
I have stuck them all together
to make one enormous bogey. It
measures 5.3 cm in diameter and
weighs 3.6 grams. Is this a record?

Yours faithfully,

Danny Baker

(Aged nine and a bit)

WARNING!
THIS STORY
MAY CONTAIN
SILLINESS

Join Danny as he attempts to smash a
load of revolting records, including:

FREE
STICKERS

LOUDEST TRUMP!
CHEESIEST FEET!
NITTIEST SCALP!

OUT NOW!

A selected list of titles available from Macmillan Children's Books

The prices shown below are correct at the time of going to press. However, Macmillan Publishers reserves the right to show new retail prices on covers, which may differ from those previously advertised.

All Pan Macmillan titles can be ordered from our website, www.panmacmillan.com, or from your local bookshop and are also available by post from:

Bookpost, PO Box 29, Douglas, Isle of Man IM99 1BQ

Credit cards accepted. For details:
Telephone: 01624 677237
Fax: 01624 670923
Email: bookshop@enterprise.net
www.bookpost.co.uk

Free postage and packing in the United Kingdom